My Furry Foster Family

Kingston the Great Dane

by Debbi Michiko Florence

illustrated by Melanie Demmer

raintree

a Capstone company — publishers for children

For two of my favourite Ks, Kalani and Kainoa — DMF

Raintree is an imprint of Capstone Global Library Limited, a company incorporated in England and Wales having its registered office at 264 Banbury Road, Oxford, OX2 7DY — Registered company number: 6695582

www.raintree.co.uk
myorders@raintree.co.uk

Text © Capstone Global Library Limited 2021
The moral rights of the proprietor have been asserted.

All rights reserved. No part of this publication may be reproduced in any form or by any means (including photocopying or storing it in any medium by electronic means and whether or not transiently or incidentally to some other use of this publication) without the written permission of the copyright owner, except in accordance with the provisions of the Copyright, Designs and Patents Act 1988 or under the terms of a licence issued by the Copyright Licensing Agency, 5th Floor, Shackleton House, 4 Battle Bridge Lane, London SE1 2HX (www.cla.co.uk). Applications for the copyright owner's written permission should be addressed to the publisher.

Edited by Jill Kalz
Designed by Lori Bye
Original illustrations © Capstone Global Library Limited 2021
Production by Tori Abraham
Originated by Capstone Global Library Ltd

Image credits
Capstone Studio: Karon Dubke, 68; Debbi Michiko Florence: 69; Melanie Demmer, 71; Roy Thomas, 70

978 1 3982 0460 7

British Library Cataloguing in Publication Data
A full catalogue record for this book is available from the British Library.

Printed in the United Kingdom

Contents

Dad
(Tim Takano)

Mum
(Cindy Takano)

Me
(Kaita Takano)

Eraser

Ollie

Joss Lawrence,
Happy Tails
Rescue

Hannah Miller,
my best friend

CHAPTER 1

Dog or cow?

My family and I foster animals. We give them love and care while they wait to find their forever homes.

Over the years, we've fostered cats, hamsters and even a bearded dragon called Betty! We've also fostered lots of dogs, of all shapes and sizes.

But none were as big as Kingston.

Kingston was a Great Dane.
He stood very tall. Next to my dog,
Ollie, Kingston looked like a calf! He
even had the same colouring as one.
He was white, with big, black spots.

Ollie is a mini dachshund. He's
a small, chubby dog who loves to eat!

The day Kingston came to our
house, I was helping my dad clean
the spare room. We keep our foster
pets in there. It's important for foster
animals to have their own space.

I was happy Kingston was coming.
But I was also worried about his size.

"I hope Kingston and Ollie get on
well," I said. "They'll be so different
from each other."

"Kingston grew up with a smaller

dog," Dad said. "And we already know that Ollie loves other dogs. I'm sure the two of them will be fine."

Yip! Yip! Yip!

"Speaking of Ollie . . . ," Dad said, smiling.

"Joss is here!" I said.

Seconds later, the doorbell rang.

Ollie always knows when someone is at the front door. He is better than a doorbell.

I ran to the door and opened it. Dad scooped up Ollie in his arms.

A woman stood in the doorway. "Hello, Mr Takano, Kaita and Ollie!" she said. It was Joss, from Happy Tails Rescue. We had adopted Ollie from Happy Tails Rescue. Now we are a foster family for them.

A huge black-and-white dog sat next to Joss.

"Takano family, meet Kingston," Joss said, holding his lead.

Kingston sat still, but his tail wagged so fast it blurred. He was cute!

"He kind of looks like a baby cow,"

I said.

"Does he moo or bark?" Dad joked.

RUFF!

"He barks!" Dad said. "OK, come on in." He opened the door wide. Ollie wagged his tail. He wriggled in Dad's arms.

Kingston walked quietly next to Joss. He didn't pull on his lead.

"He heels quite well," Dad said.

Joss chuckled. "Yes, he does," she said. "A dog this size needs to be well trained. Kingston has very good manners. He learns quickly."

Ollie wanted to meet Kingston. Dad put Ollie on the floor.

"Kingston, down," Joss said.

Kingston lay down. Even lying down, his head was higher than Ollie standing up!

Ollie walked over and greeted Kingston. The two dogs sniffed each other. They wagged their tails.

Joss unclipped the lead. Kingston walked over to me. His head came up to my shoulder.

"Wow, he's super-tall!" I said as he sniffed my ear. His nose tickled. I giggled.

Kingston turned to my dad. His tail wagged even faster. He stood on his hind legs and put his front paws on Dad's shoulders. It was like they were dancing!

I laughed. Dad did too.

"Maybe Kingston thinks you look like his former owner," Joss said.

"What happened to his owner?" I asked.

"He had to sell his house and move into an apartment," Joss said.

"Oh. Was Kingston too big for the apartment?" I asked.

"Yes," Joss said. "The owner was very sad about having to give him up. He was able to keep his other, much smaller dog, though. A small dog will work well in an apartment."

Dad petted Kingston and told him he was a good boy. Kingston liked that. He dropped back down to the floor and sat.

"Thank you again for fostering

Kingston," Joss said. "It was hard to find a family with enough space. Also, it's nice that you already have a dog. I'm sure Kingston misses his dog friend."

Dad went to Joss' truck to get the rest of the supplies. I stayed with Kingston. He gave me a happy grin and wagged his tail.

"We're going to have so much fun, Kingston," I said. "We will find the perfect home for you."

CHAPTER 2

Just like Ollie

My mum came home from her job at the bookshop later that day. Mum made friends with Kingston straight away. Our new foster dog seemed to love everyone!

Like Joss said, Kingston had good manners. While we ate our soup, Ollie slept under my chair. Kingston stretched out next to Dad. He made himself at home.

Before bedtime, I read for a little while. Ollie curled up next to me on my bed. Kingston lay down on the floor. I read out loud so both dogs got a bedtime story. Kingston was so good. Mum and Dad let him sleep in my room that night.

The next morning, Kingston decided that Ollie was his new best friend. Kingston followed him everywhere. And I mean *everywhere*.

I set the table for breakfast while Dad made pancakes. Mum got back from her morning run. Just before we sat down to eat, Ollie went under my chair. He always does that during mealtimes.

Kingston followed.

Yip! Yip! Yip! Ollie shot out from under my chair.

"What's going on?" Mum asked.

Mum, Dad and I watched as my chair went up . . . up . . . up! Kingston was wearing it like a hat!

"I think Kingston was trying to go under Kaita's chair, like Ollie does," Dad said, grinning.

Kingston tilted his head. The chair fell to the floor. I put the chair back by the table and gave Kingston a hug.

"Kingston, you're too big to fit under my chair," I said.

Dad told Kingston to sit next to him. Ollie went back to his spot under my chair. And Dad, Mum and I got stuck into our pancakes.

After breakfast, Ollie, Kingston and I went to my room. I lifted Ollie onto my bed.

"Kingston, you sit here, next to my bed," I said, pointing to the rug. "I want to draw your picture."

I got my sketchbook and pencils. I like to draw pictures of our foster pets. It's a fun way to remember them after they find their forever homes.

RUFF!

Yip! Yip! Yip!

Oops! Kingston stepped up onto my bed next to Ollie. He took up the whole thing! Imagine if you had a baby cow on your bed! Ollie scooted backwards onto my pillow.

I laughed. "Oh, Ollie, I think Kingston wants to do everything you do!" I said.

I moved Ollie from my bed to the floor. Kingston stepped down off my bed. He watched Ollie to see what he would do next.

Ollie picked up his tennis ball. Kingston sniffed the ball and made a snuffling sound. Ollie is a good foster brother, but he doesn't like to share his favourite toy. He ran out of my room with his ball and down the hall.

RUFF! Kingston galloped after him.

I followed both dogs into the living room. Mum and Dad were sitting on the sofa. Dad was reading. Mum was knitting.

Ollie pawed Mum's legs. She picked him up and put him on her lap. He still had his ball in his mouth.

Kingston stopped in the middle of the room, his tail wagging. He looked at little Ollie sitting on Mum's lap. Then he looked at Dad.

"Now what are you going to do?" I asked Kingston. "You're much too big for the sofa."

Kingston stared at Dad for a bit. Then he shook his head and turned around to face me.

RUFF!

And just like that, the big Great Dane slowly backed away from me, step by step. When he was right in front of my dad, he folded his back legs and sat down! His front legs were still on the floor, but the rest of him was sitting on Dad's lap!

We all burst out laughing.

"Well, look! Kingston is a lap dog, just like Ollie," Dad said.

"How funny!" Mum said. "Sweet Kingston, you really have no idea how big you are, do you?"

Kingston looked very happy as Dad petted him. He even drooled a little.

"He's got the body of a Great Dane and the heart of a mini dachshund," I said, giggling.

Ollie dropped his tennis ball and wriggled. Mum put him back on the floor. He ran to the kitchen door.

Yip! Yip! Yip!

Seconds later, someone knocked. Dad held on to Kingston's collar so he couldn't follow.

"Hannah must be here!" I said, racing to the kitchen.

My best friend loves to come to my house. She *really* loves to come over whenever we get a new foster pet. I had told Hannah we were getting a Great Dane.

I opened the door and pulled her into the house.

"Come and meet Kingston," I said. "You're going to love him!"

CHAPTER 3

A hurting paw

I was right. Hannah loved
Kingston the minute she met him.
He loved her too.

Hannah and I went into the
garden with the dogs. Hannah played
fetch with Kingston. I played fetch
with Ollie. I really like having foster
pets, but I always make sure Ollie
never feels left out.

Yip! Yip! Yip! Ollie chased his favourite tennis ball. He brought it back. I threw it again.

Hannah threw a rope toy with knots. It was Kingston's favourite toy. He ran after it and brought it back. The dogs never seemed to get tired of the game.

"My arm hurts from throwing," Hannah said after a while.

"Mine too!" I said, rubbing my arm.

We took a break and watched Ollie and Kingston run around the garden. When they finally *did* get tired, Ollie flopped down by my feet. He chewed on his ball. Kingston sniffed some flowers in Mum's garden.

Suddenly, Kingston yelped. *YOWL!*
He backed away quickly from the
flowers and held up his front paw.

"He's hurt!" Hannah cried.

"Quick! Get my mum!" I said.

I ran over to Kingston and put out my hand. He let me take his hurt paw. I didn't see anything wrong with it. He wasn't bleeding.

Seconds later, Mum and Hannah came outside. Mum took a look at Kingston and then at her flower bed. "Bees really love these flowers," she said. "I think he got stung. Poor guy. Let's take him to see Rhonda."

Rhonda is our vet. *Vet* is short for *veterinarian*. That's a doctor for animals. Rhonda's the best. I want to be a vet like her one day.

Hannah had a piano lesson, so she couldn't come with us. Dad took her home. Mum and I took Kingston to the vet's surgery.

When we take Ollie there, he hides behind my legs or shakes in my arms. Even though Rhonda is nice, Ollie doesn't like seeing her.

Kingston, on the other hand, seemed very happy at the vet's surgery. Even with his hurt paw, he wagged his tail. He limped to the scale and stepped up.

"Sit, Kingston," I said.

Kingston sat and got weighed. Wow! It would take fifteen Ollies to weigh as much as one Kingston!

Mum and I took Kingston into a room. It had a metal table, a counter and two chairs. Kingston didn't seem to be limping as much any more.

Rhonda walked in a few minutes later. She wore a white lab coat with pockets. A stethoscope hung around her neck. Rhonda always wears her blonde hair in a ponytail. I like her because she is always smiling.

"Hi, Cindy. Hi, Kaita. Who do we have here?" Rhonda asked.

"This is Kingston," I said. "We're fostering him. He hurt his paw. Mum thinks a bee stung him."

Kingston wagged his tail and greeted Rhonda.

"He's a very happy dog," she said.

Kingston didn't move at all as Rhonda listened to his heart with her stethoscope. She checked his eyes, ears, nose and teeth. Kingston sat still. I was proud of him.

Rhonda took his front paw in her hand. She looked closely. Kingston stopped wagging his tail, but he didn't pull away.

"I don't see a stinger in here, so that's good news," Rhonda said. "Kaita, did you see a bee sting Kingston?"

"No," I said. "I just heard him yelp."

"He was sniffing in my flower bed, and there are a lot of bees there," Mum said.

"Well, there is only a little swelling," Rhonda said. "I'm going to give him some medicine. It will make the swelling go down."

Rhonda left the room for a few minutes. Kingston wagged his tail, and I hugged him.

"He is such a great dog," Mum said. "I'm sure he will find a wonderful home."

When Rhonda came back, she waved a green treat. Kingston trotted over to her and ate it up.

Rhonda laughed. "Works every time," she said. "That was a treat that hides pills. We just put the pill inside. Dogs don't even know they are eating medicine."

"Cool!" I said.

"Big boy Kingston will be fine," Rhonda said. "But if his paw swells up more, or if he seems in pain, please call us."

I was so happy Kingston was OK!

CHAPTER 4

Indoor games

Every day after school, Mum and I took Ollie and Kingston for a walk to the dog park. Dogs get to run around off their leads there. They meet and play with all kinds of other dogs. They love it!

Kingston went everywhere Ollie went. They raced from one corner of the park to the other.

Most days, Mum took Ollie into our garden afterwards, while she gardened. Kingston usually sat with me in the house while I drew or read. His paw was fine, but he didn't like playing fetch in the garden much any more. I think he was afraid he'd get stung again.

"Do you want to play a game, Kingston?" I asked one day. "It's called Find It." I picked up his rope toy. Kingston walked over to me. He wagged his tail.

"Sit," I said.

Kingston sat.

"Stay," I said. This was a trick Kingston was very good at. He would stay until I said it was OK to move.

I walked out of the kitchen and into my room. I put the toy on my bed. Then I went back to the kitchen.

"OK, Kingston, find it!" I said. I had seen a game like this on TV.

Kingston stood up. He nudged my arm. I showed him my hands.

"I don't have it," I said. "Find your rope toy, Kingston! Find it!"

Kingston wagged his tail. *RUFF!* He barked in my face. I laughed.

"Come with me," I said. "I'll show you how it's done."

Kingston followed me to my room. He saw his toy straight away. He ran to my bed and grabbed the toy in his mouth. He wagged his tail and danced around my room.

"Good boy," I said, taking the toy from him. "Now you know how the game is played. Let's try it again. Ready? Sit."

Kingston sat.

"Stay," I said.

I walked to the living room and put his rope toy on the sofa. Then I went back to my room.

Kingston was still sitting and waiting. He wagged his tail.

"OK, find it!" I said.

Kingston took off down the hallway and raced in to the living room. I ran after him. I watched him quickly sniff each chair, then the sofa. He found his toy! He learnt so fast. He was one clever dog.

We played Find It all afternoon. When Dad came home from work, I showed him the new game.

"That's great, Kaita," Dad said. "Hey, guess what?"

Dad smiled and raised his eyebrows. His eyes looked happy. I knew what that look on his face meant. I'd seen it many times before. My heart did a little pitter-patter.

"Is someone thinking about adopting Kingston?" I asked.

This is part of being a foster family. And it's a tough part. The most important thing is finding good homes for the foster pets. Even so, I always feel a little sad when we have to say goodbye.

"Yes, but Joss said there are *two* people interested in him," Dad said. "Joss has approved them both."

"Wow!" I said. Usually only one person at a time is approved to adopt a pet. "How is that going to work?"

"The first person, Amy, is a university student," Dad said. "Joss thinks Amy would show Kingston a lot of love. But she's worried that Amy might not have enough time to spend with him. It sounds like Amy has a lot of studies to do."

Like Joss, I worried too. Kingston needed time for play and exercise. He loved to go for walks and spend time at the dog park.

Dad continued. "Another person, Liam, showed interest in Kingston at the same time," he said. "Liam already has a dog, so Joss thought he'd be a good fit."

"Kingston could have a dog friend, like Ollie!" I added.

"Right," Dad said. "So, Amy will come over on Saturday morning. Liam will come over in the afternoon. Then, Joss will speak to both of them and make a decision."

Having two people interested in Kingston was amazing! We all wanted Kingston to have the very best home to make him happy.

CHAPTER 5

A choice to make

On Saturday morning, I brushed Kingston. He had short hair that didn't really need to be brushed. But he seemed to like it. I kneeled down and straightened his collar. I gave him a big hug. He licked the top of my head.

"OK, Kingston," I whispered in his ear. "Let's get you a wonderful new family and home."

Mum and Ollie went to the dog park so Amy could meet Kingston alone. Kingston loved Ollie so much. We wanted to make sure Kingston paid attention just to Amy.

The doorbell rang. It was strange not to have Ollie bark beforehand.

Dad opened the door and greeted Amy. She had black hair just like me.

"Hello, Amy," Dad said. "Please, come on in."

Amy smiled. "Hi! So, where is Kingston the Great Dane?" she asked.

RUFF!

Kingston trotted into the room. His ears perked up when he first saw Amy. He wagged his tail and went straight over to her.

Amy giggled as he sniffed her face. She patted his head. "You remind me of my first dog," she said. Amy turned to me and Dad. "I had a Great Dane when I was a little girl."

"Kingston has good manners," I said. I showed Amy all the great things he could do, like sit and stay. "He also heels when he's on a lead."

Dad invited Amy to sit on the sofa. I sat on the floor. Kingston looked at Dad. Then he looked at Amy. He turned around and walked backwards. As always, he sat on Dad's lap. Amy laughed.

"He seems a little big to be a lap dog," she said.

"Kingston, come here," I said. I didn't want Amy to think that Kingston would do that all the time. Besides, he only sat on Dad.

Kingston walked over and sat down next to me.

"He is a sweetheart," Amy said. "Thank you both for the visit. I hope I get approved to take him home with me."

And just like that, Amy stood up to go. I was surprised she didn't have any questions. None! Dad was surprised too.

"Did you have any questions about Kingston?" Dad asked.

"No, not really," Amy said. "He seems perfect."

"He loves other dogs," I offered. "We take him to the dog park almost every day."

Amy frowned. "Oh, do I have to take him to a dog park?" she asked. "I have a lot of studying to do."

Dad shook his head. "No, I'm sure he'd be just as happy with a couple of walks and a little playtime each day."

"I could try and do two walks a day, but I don't know," Amy said. "I'm sure it'll work out. But I have to get going now. I have an exam coming up. Thanks again!"

After Amy left, I hugged Kingston. He wagged his tail.

"What did you think of Amy, Kaita?" Dad asked.

I shrugged. "She was OK, I guess. She didn't seem very interested in Kingston, though. I mean, she liked him, but she didn't ask a lot of questions about how to make him happy."

"I thought the same thing," Dad said. "Let's see what happens with Liam."

When the doorbell rang after lunch, Mum and Ollie were in the garden. Joss had told us that Liam already had a dog. He was bringing the dog with him to our house. He wanted to see if she and Kingston would get along.

A tall man wearing glasses walked into our house.

"Hello," Dad said. "Welcome!"

"Hi! I'm Liam, and this is Trixie," the man said. He held a little black-and-white terrier in his arms.

"They're the same colours!" I said, pointing to Trixie and Kingston.

Kingston sat by the sofa. His tongue hung out of his mouth. That was the way he smiled.

"Can I put down my dog?" Liam asked. "She loves other dogs."

"Yes, that's fine," I said.

Liam put Trixie on the floor. She ran straight over to Kingston. The two dogs sniffed each other. They wagged their tails.

RUFF! Kingston bowed to Trixie. That meant he wanted to play.

Woof, woof! Trixie jumped up on Kingston and wagged her tail fast. Kingston rolled over. It was funny and cute.

Liam and Dad sat on the sofa and talked while the two dogs played.

"I can tell that Kingston likes dogs," Liam said. "Is he friendly with people outside your family?"

Kingston stopped playing and looked at Liam. It was like he understood Liam's question. Kingston turned round and slowly reversed. This time, though, he didn't sit on Dad's lap. This time, Kingston sat on Liam's lap!

Dad laughed. "I think he likes you, Liam," he said.

"This is fantastic," Liam said with a big smile. "A giant lap dog!"

Liam asked Dad and me a lot of questions. He wanted to know what Kingston liked and didn't like. He asked if Kingston would be OK being alone with another dog. Liam worked during the day, and he wanted Trixie to have a friend.

"Kingston has good manners," Dad said. "We leave him alone in the house when we are out. He never gets into trouble."

I showed Liam how Kingston played Find It. Guess what? Trixie knew how to play too!

When it was time for Liam and Trixie to leave, Liam gave Kingston a hug. "I think you would be perfect for our family," he said.

I thought so too. Dad agreed.

Later, when Joss called to ask us what we thought, Dad told her everything. Then we waited.

Finally, on Sunday afternoon, Joss called us with the news. Kingston would be going home with Liam. Amy had changed her mind and decided she wasn't ready for a dog. I hoped that one day she would find her perfect pet. For now, I was happy that Kingston was going to live with Liam and Trixie.

Helping foster pets find their forever homes is the best!

Think about it!

1. Kingston loves Ollie. What are some things he does to copy Ollie?
2. Kaita didn't see how Kingston got hurt. What clues did Kaita and her mum use to guess what happened to him?
3. What do you think it would be like to be a vet? What would you like and dislike about the job?

Draw it! Write it!

1. Draw a picture of Kingston and Ollie playing in a paddling pool. Remember, Kingston is much bigger than Ollie!
2. Write a letter to Joss. Tell her why you think Amy or Liam should adopt Kingston. Include examples of the things they did and said to support your choice.

Glossary

adopt take and raise as one's own

dachshund type of dog with a long body and short legs

former having once been something that it isn't now

foster give care and a safe home for a short time

heel walk closely to a handler's heel

stethoscope piece of medical equipment that includes a disc and two earpieces, used to listen to someone's heart

terrier small breed of dog that usually has a lot of energy

vet person trained to take care of the health of animals

yelp short, sharp cry, usually of pain or surprise

What do you want to be?

Kaita Takano is a made-up character in the My Furry Foster Family series. But she is based on a real-life Kaita.

The two Kaitas are alike in some ways. They both foster pets and have a mini dachshund called Ollie. But the girls are different in some ways too. Story Kaita is eight years old and Japanese American. Real Kaita is ten years old and half Korean American, half European American.

So, what does Story Kaita want to be when she grows up? A vet! Like Rhonda in this story, a vet has a room where animals go for check-ups. If the animals are ill or hurt, they get medicine or sometimes they are looked after overnight at the vet's.

How do you become a vet?

You must love animals and science! Vets go to university for a number of years.

What kinds of animals do vets look after?

Vets may focus their studies on small or large animals. Small animals may include dogs, cats and birds. Large ones may include cows, horses and pigs. Some vets look after pets or other domesticated animals. Others look after wild ones.

What does Real Kaita want to be when she grows up? Author Debbi Michiko Florence asked her!

K: I enjoy doing so many things. It's hard to decide! A downhill skier? Clothing designer? I guess I most want to be a manga artist because I absolutely love manga and anime*. I love to draw and design characters.

*Manga is a Japanese or Japanese-style graphic novel or comic book. Anime is animation (like a film) based on manga.

KAITA

HANNAH

A long time ago, I wanted to be a daschund trainer. But then I learnt that daschunds don't listen. Ha! Did you always want to be a writer, Debbi?

DMF: No, not exactly. I always loved to write (and read) stories, but when I was young, I didn't think of writing as a job. The other thing I loved was animals. For a long time, I wanted to be a vet. I even went to university and got a degree in zoology (the study of animals). It wasn't until I got married that I decided to become a writer. I love writing books!

· Chemistry·
BIOLOGY
ZOOLOGY

Reader, what do you want to be when you grow up? Why?

About the author

Debbi Michiko Florence writes books for children in her writing studio, The Word Nest. She is an animal lover with a degree in zoology and has worked at a pet shop, the Humane Society, a raptor rehabilitation centre and a zoo. She is the author of two chapter book series: Jasmine Toguchi and Dorothy & Toto. Debbi lives in Connecticut, USA, with her husband, a rescue dog, a rabbit and two ducks.

About the illustrator

Melanie Demmer is an illustrator and designer living in Los Angeles, USA. She graduated with a BFA in illustration from the College for Creative Studies in Detroit and has been creating artwork for various clothing, animation and publishing projects ever since. When she isn't making art, Melanie enjoys writing, spending time in the great outdoors, iced tea, scary films and having naps with her cat, Pepper.

Go on all the fun, furry foster adventures!

Apple and Annie, the Hamster Duo

Betty the Bearded Dragon

Buttons the Kitten

Kingston the Great Dane

Murray the Ferret

Roo the Rabbit

Tiki the Cockatoo

Toby the Dog

Only from Raintree!